MYSTERY

D0441960

The Haunted Mansion Mystery

Want to read more of Barbie's Mystery Files? Don't miss the second book in the series, *The Mystery of the Jeweled Mask.*

MYSTERY FILES #1

The Haunted Mansion Mystery

By Linda Aber

SCHOLASTIC INC.

New York   Toronto   London   Auckland   Sydney
Mexico City   New Delhi   Hong Kong   Buenos Aires

ISBN 0-439-37204-6

Designed by Peter Koblish
Photography by Paul Jordan, Mary Reveles, Jake Johnson, Mark Adams, Lisa Collins, and Judy Tsuno

12 11 10 9 8 7 6 5 4 3 2   2 3 4 5 6 7/0

Printed in the U.S.A.
First Scholastic printing, January 2002

You can help Barbie solve this mystery! Flip to page 52 and use the reporter's notebook to jot down facts, clues, and suspects in the case. Add more notes as you and Barbie uncover clues. If you can figure out who the culprit is, you'll be on your way to becoming a star reporter, just like Barbie!

Barbie™

MYSTERY FILES #1

The Haunted Mansion Mystery

Chapter 1

●●●●●●●●●●●●●●●●●●●

A TOUGH ASSIGNMENT

"Whew!" Barbie breathed. She set her tote bag down by the chair Becky was saving for her. "This is the first break I've had all day!"

"And you're right on time," said Becky. "As usual! I ordered chicken salad sandwiches and lemonade for both of us."

"Perfect!" Barbie smiled.

The two young women had been friends ever since they were in the second grade. They had even gone to the same college. Now Barbie was a reporter and Becky worked as a researcher at the Willow History Museum.

The Willow Café, on the main street of the town, was always crowded at lunch hour. Several people waved to Barbie as they spotted her coming inside. Barbie had lived in Willow all her life. She was well known even before she became a reporter for the town's oldest newspaper, the *Willow Gazette.*

"I'm so glad I could talk you into taking time out to have lunch with me," Becky said. "Even a newspaper reporter has to eat, right?"

"Sure I do!" Barbie laughed. She took a bite of the sandwich and sipped her lemonade. "But lunch is my treat today. It's the least I can do to thank you for all the help you've given me with my story on the Willow family and the one-hundredth Willow Founder's Day celebration in two weeks. What an interesting family history the Willows have!"

Becky smiled at her tall blond friend. She liked that Barbie found so many things interesting. That was what made her a great reporter and also a great friend. "I'm glad I could help you, Barbie," Becky said. "How is the story coming along?"

The look on Barbie's face turned serious. She reached into the tote bag and pulled out her reporter's notebook. Barbie noticed the man at the next table listening. She didn't want to be overheard, so she lowered her voice. "What began as a simple assignment," she said softly, "is turning out to be a lot tougher than I expected."

"How so?" Becky asked.

"I got off to a great start, but now I'm stuck," Barbie replied. "This is what I have so far." Barbie read from her notebook. "The town of Willow was founded one hundred years ago by Mr. Fielding Willow, a respected botanist. He experimented with plants. The town was named for him after he created the Fielding rose."

"Oh!" said Becky. "The Fielding rose is beautiful."

"It's more than just beautiful," Barbie explained. "There's something special about the Fielding rose. It's able to bloom all year-round, no matter what the temperature is."

"Wow!" Becky exclaimed. "How can it? Roses usually bloom in the warmer months."

Barbie's eyes lit up with excitement. "That's the interesting part of the story. Just before Fielding Willow was about to share his information with other scientists, he died unexpectedly. Unfortunately, his secret died with him."

"And nobody knows the secret?" Becky asked.

Barbie shook her head. "Nobody. Fielding Wil-

3

low was a very private man. After he created the Fielding rose, the public attention was too much for him. He chose to stay out of the spotlight. That's one reason I wanted to talk to Fielding Willow's grandson, Alfred Willow. I was hoping he'd be able to tell me more about his grandfather and the work he did."

"Alfred Willow is a charming gentleman!" Becky said. "I've met him several times at the museum. He lives at Willow's Way, the estate on the edge of town. I'm sure he'd be glad to talk with you."

Barbie looked troubled. "I'm afraid he doesn't want to talk with me at all," she said. "At first he seemed very interested in speaking with me. We made an appointment for tomorrow morning. But when I called today, Mr. Willow sounded nervous on the phone. He said he was sorry, but he had changed his mind about the interview."

"Hmm," Becky said. "I'm surprised to hear that. Maybe he was having a bad day. Or maybe he's nervous because you're a stranger to him. He's elderly and lives alone. Why don't I call him and see if I can arrange for a visit from both of us?"

"Thanks, Becky," Barbie said. "You're a real friend."

While Barbie paid the check, Becky made the phone call. "Good news!" she said when she returned. "Mr. Willow will see us tomorrow morning at nine A.M.! He seemed unsure at first, but when I told him we'd been friends forever, he agreed to meet."

"Fantastic!" Barbie exclaimed. "Nine A.M. tomorrow, Willow's Way. I'll pick you up."

As the two friends were saying their good-byes, they were startled by a shout from the waitress who had waited on them. "Hey!" the woman called after the man who had been sitting at the next table. He was rushing out the door. "You dropped something!"

Thinking fast, Barbie ran to the door to catch the man before he got too far. She caught a glimpse of a man with dark hair and a medium build hopping on a bus.

"I'm sorry," Barbie said when she came back inside the café. "I missed him."

"Oh, well," the waitress said. "It was only this. He dropped it on his way out. I wasn't sure if it might be important." She handed Barbie a napkin with writing on it.

Barbie's eyes widened as she read the words on the paper. "Nine A.M. tomorrow, Willow's Way."

"Becky," Barbie said slowly, "whoever he was, I have a hunch that man was listening to everything we were saying!"

"But why?" Becky asked.

"Good question, Becky," Barbie replied. "A very good question indeed!"

Chapter 2

SOMETHING STRANGE AT WILLOW'S WAY

Becky was already outside when Barbie arrived in her shiny red convertible. "Isn't this a perfect day to put the top down on the car?" Barbie said, smiling.

"It sure is," Becky replied. "The gardens at Willow's Way will look lovely today."

Barbie helped Becky into the car. Becky had always used a wheelchair, but Barbie hardly even noticed it anymore. She folded it up and fit it neatly into the trunk. "Okay," Barbie said as she got in and fastened her seat belt. "Willow's Way, here we come!"

In less than fifteen minutes, the two friends saw the sign for the Willow estate. Barbie turned left and drove slowly up the long, tree-lined drive. Remembering the stranger in the Willow Café, Barbie almost expected to see him hiding behind one of the trees. Of course, the man was nowhere in sight.

Even before they reached the stately yellow house at the top of the drive, the girls could see a colorful garden full of roses. As they got closer, they were surprised at what else was in the garden.

"Weeds!" Barbie cried. "What a shame to let things get so overgrown." Clearly, it had been quite a while since any yard work had been done.

Barbie parked the car and the two girls got out. As they approached the wide front door, they saw movement around the corner of the house. A man in work clothes was bent over a garden. Barbie stopped in her tracks. *Is it the man from the café?* she wondered. He didn't look up from his work. He was pulling out weeds and pressing the soil down again around the most beautiful flowers they had ever seen. It was a garden full of the famous Fielding roses. "Aren't they lovely?" Becky gasped.

"Yes, they are," Barbie agreed. "And I'm glad to see that Mr. Willow has a gardener," she added softly. "But there's certainly too much work here for one person. He could really use some help."

The porch of the old mansion was creaky and cobwebby. It was clear that the house had seen better times. It was still beautiful, but it had an air of neglect that made it seem a little creepy.

Barbie rang the doorbell. The heavy door swung slowly open. An elderly white-haired man peered around the door. "Yes?" he said nervously.

"Good morning, Mr. Willow," Becky replied. "It's so nice to see you again. I'd like you to meet my good friend Barbie Roberts."

The gentleman opened the door wider. "Hello, Becky." He turned to Barbie and said softly, "I apologize for my poor manners. I'm just not myself lately. Please come in."

Barbie and Becky entered a grand foyer. A sweet and musty odor filled the air. It wasn't unpleasant, but it was definitely strange. Always the reporter, Barbie made a mental note of the air and the thick layer of dust on the table. The inside was even creepier than the outside.

"Pardon the dust, please," Mr. Willow said sadly. "My housekeeper left suddenly."

9

"Oh, but the wallpaper and the drawings are beautiful!" Barbie said, changing the subject. Pen-and-ink drawings of all kinds of flowers lined the walls. "Who is the artist?"

"My grandfather, Fielding Willow," the gentleman replied. "You'll see many of his works on all three floors of the house. Grandfather built the house in stages. It began as a small one-story house built right on top of the land. As Grandfather's success grew, so did the house. I believe the original plans are in your museum, Becky," he said. "Although I myself have never seen them."

Mr. Willow led his two visitors through a sitting room, a dining room, and a living room. Each room had a different flowered wallpaper. "As you can see," Mr. Willow explained, "my grandfather had a great fascination with flowers."

"I've never seen wallpaper like this before," Barbie exclaimed.

"No," Mr. Willow agreed. "And you won't see it again, I'm sorry to say. The wallpapers are also my grandfather's original designs." He led Barbie and Becky to a drawing room bordered in iris flowers of all colors.

"The flowers inside are as beautiful as the ones outside," Barbie said.

A sad look came over Mr. Willow's face. His blue eyes clouded over, and he was clearly troubled.

"I'm sorry," Barbie said. "I hope I haven't said something to upset you."

"Oh, no, miss," he said sadly. "You are right. The gardens are beautiful. I hope I am able to keep them groomed. My regular gardening staff left at the same time my housekeeper did."

"What a shame," Becky said.

"Yes," Mr. Willow went on. "I've had to take on this new fellow to handle all the grounds. He seems knowledgeable and showed up just at the right time. I only hope he won't be scared off, too!"

Barbie and Becky exchanged worried looks. Barbie tried to lighten the mood with happier talk of the upcoming Founder's Day celebration. She opened her notebook and took careful notes as Mr. Willow told his family's history. He spoke with great pride of his grandfather's work. "The only low point in his life," Mr. Willow explained, "was near the end. He had a falling-out with his assistant."

"A falling-out?" Barbie asked.

11

Mr. Willow nodded. "A young man named Carl Axel was his aide. Grandfather discovered that Carl was selling his formulas to an independent laboratory. He fired Carl, and soon after, he became very ill. Of course, you know Grandfather died just before he finished his last and most important study."

THUD! THUD! THUD! Suddenly, Mr. Willow's story was interrupted by a loud noise echoing through the vents in the floor. Becky, Barbie, and Mr. Willow all jumped at the sound. Before anyone could say anything, the noise stopped. "Do you have a houseguest?" Barbie asked.

"Oh, it's much worse than that," the gentleman whispered nervously. "It's more like a house *ghost*! That's why the housekeeper and the groundskeepers left. They believe my house is haunted!"

"Haunted?" Becky and Barbie gasped together.

Mr. Willow leaned in closer. "I tried to assure them that it's just the old furnace knocking. But sometimes I'm not so sure," he breathed. "I've heard other sounds as well. Footsteps. Voices. Sometimes a strong odor seems to come from nowhere in Grandfather's study." A frightened look spread over his face. "I'm sure it's just my imagination. But I can't help feeling that someone or some*thing* wants me to leave Willow's Way."

"But who?" Barbie asked. "And why?"

"I don't know the answers to your questions," Mr. Willow said. "And I'm feeling very tired now. Do you mind if we continue another time?"

"Of course," Barbie replied. "Becky needs to get back to the museum, and I have to use the library. But I would like to look into the strange events here at Willow's Way. Maybe you would let us come back tomorrow afternoon? We could do a little investigating and help out in your garden, too!"

"We'd love to!" Becky added.

Mr. Willow smiled for the first time that day. "That would be wonderful!" he said gratefully. "Until tomorrow, then."

As Mr. Willow led them to the front door, Becky smiled at Barbie, who was already deep in thought. Becky knew her friend very well. Barbie liked gardening, but she *loved* a mystery.

Chapter 3

• • • • • • • • • • • • • • • • • • • •

THE CLUE IN THE MUSEUM

The Willow History Museum had just been re-painted in honor of the Founder's Day celebration. The fresh yellow clapboard and green shutters matched the house at Willow's Way. Barbie and Becky went inside together.

"I have to catch up on my work," said Becky. "But you know your way around our library." She led Barbie to a large room lined with bookshelves, file drawers, and tables with study lamps. "I'll see you later." Becky left Barbie on her own.

Agnes, the librarian, was on the phone. She covered the mouthpiece and whispered to Barbie, "Just ask if you need anything."

"Will do," Barbie said. "Thanks!"

In fact, Barbie knew right where the Willow files

14

were. She kept her notebook handy and jotted down facts she thought would be important for her story. She learned that the house was designed and built by Fielding Willow in 1870. A floor plan of the house showed many rooms. But she was surprised to find a basement area marked LABORATORY. Hadn't Mr. Willow said that the house was built right on top of the land?

Barbie looked through several other files. The one she was most interested in was missing. In its place was a sign-out card. Someone named Violet Langley had already checked out the Fielding Willow's formulas file several days before.

"Agnes?" Barbie said as soon as the librarian was off the phone. "I'm afraid I do need something. The Fielding Willow's formulas file has already been signed out. May I put my name on the waiting list?"

"Yes, of course," Agnes replied. "But someone else was just in here asking about the same file. He put his name on the list first. John Lexa."

"Oh, dear," Barbie said. "I was hoping to get a look at the file for my newspaper story. Would it be possible for you to call him? I'd like to ask if he'd mind letting me look at the file before he takes it."

"I'd be glad to do that, Barbie," Agnes replied. "There's just one problem. Mr. Lexa didn't leave a number. He said he'd stop by to check on the file."

Barbie thanked Agnes and left the library. On her way out of the museum, she stopped to look in a glass display case. It was filled with things that had belonged to Fielding Willow. There were old photos of Fielding with his prize roses. Next to the photos was a letter from the Academy of Botany congratulating Fielding Willow on his creation of the new Fielding rose. At the back of the case, a leather diary was opened to a page with Fielding Willow's handwriting. Barbie leaned closer to get a better look at it. The first few lines looked like a formula for something. It was written in a neat and steady hand.

Fielding Formula Part 1

Soil N   Soil Test Potassium, p

Yield N Bray-I 0-40   41-80 81-120 121-160   161+

Nitrogen recommendation $= 0.05$ YG - STN* + SDA − PCC

(Bray-I) Phosphate recommendation $= (0.0225 - 0.0011$ STP$)$YG

* * *

Barbie skimmed over the notes and concentrated on what was written below them. In a much shakier hand, the lines read:

I am ill. The experiment is just days from completion. Until I am well, part 2 of my formula shall be safe where roses grow and warm breezes blow. — FW

Of course, Barbie had already heard about Fielding Willow's illness and the unfinished experiment. But she was curious about the last line. She copied the words into her reporter's notebook. *"Part 2 of my formula shall be safe where roses grow and warm breezes blow."*

"'. . . Where roses grow and warm breezes blow,'" Barbie repeated slowly. Suddenly, she realized there was something else she needed to look up in the library. She went back and was surprised to see a man bending over the file drawer. He looked familiar. Barbie stepped behind a bookshelf and watched him for a few seconds. Even bending over, he looked tall. His feet were bigger than average, and his shoulders were broad. Barbie tried to remember where she'd seen him. As

Barbie watched, the man closed the file drawer and went to the desk.

"Good afternoon, ma'am," he said to Agnes. "I'm looking for the file on Fielding Willow's formulas."

Agnes chuckled. "It's signed out," she told him. "I'd be glad to add your name to the waiting list, but don't hold your breath. There are a couple of folks ahead of you!"

"Yes, add my name to the list, please," the man said politely. "It's Kip Mackenzie."

Barbie hadn't heard the name before. She didn't have the chance to come out from behind the shelf to see his face. The man left without looking back. *Kip Mackenzie.* She added his name to her notebook along with the names Violet Langley and John Lexa.

Three strangers interested in Fielding Willow's formulas, Barbie thought. *It seems the more I find out, the more there is to know!*

Chapter 4

• •

A SURPRISE IN THE SHED

Barbie and Becky rang Mr. Willow's doorbell the next afternoon. They were dressed in gardening clothes. When Mr. Willow answered the door, his eyes were red and he was very pale. His hands shook as he ran them through his uncombed hair.

"Oh, Mr. Willow!" Barbie gasped. "Are you ill?"

"Come in," the man said with some relief. "I've been awake all night. I thought I heard footsteps and noises again. Perhaps I was dreaming."

"Have you called the police?" Barbie asked.

"No!" Mr. Willow sputtered. "No police! With the Founder's Day celebration coming there'll be enough publicity already. I don't want to spoil the event with police reports and bad news stories." He stepped outside and joined the girls on the path. "Please," he continued, "let's not speak of

19

this anymore. I feel better just seeing your bright faces."

"We feel lucky to be in the midst of such lovely gardens," Becky said cheerfully. Both she and Barbie tried not to look as worried as they really were.

"Please promise me you won't overdo it," Mr. Willow said. "You must come in for lemonade the second you feel tired."

"We will," Barbie promised. "I also want to continue our discussion from yesterday. I have a few questions for my story."

Mr. Willow smiled weakly. "Oh, many people have had many questions over the years," he sighed. "But folks lost interest until this Founder's Day celebration."

"Yes, I've noticed that," Barbie said, thinking of the list of people waiting to get a look at Fielding Willow's file. As a cloud moved slowly over the sun, she brought the subject back to the work at hand. "We'd better get busy out here, though, before the weather changes. Do you have gardening tools for us to use?"

"I'm sure you'll find everything you need in the

garden shed," Mr. Willow said. He pointed to a large work shed sheltered by a hedge behind the house.

As Barbie and Becky made their way down the path to the shed, Barbie glanced back at the old house. There was something ominous about it, even in the sunlight. Barbie wasn't suspicious, but she couldn't help shivering.

The shed was much bigger than they had expected. "It's more like a garden house than a shed," Becky commented.

The door was open. Gardening tools hung neatly on one wall. Bags of seed and fertilizer were stacked against another wall. A pair of very large work boots stood by the door. The girls went inside to pick out the things they'd need. They were surprised to see a tall blond young man adjusting a heat lamp over a flat of plant seedlings. The man was so intent on his work, he didn't hear them come in. Barbie cleared her throat.

"Oh!" the man gasped. "Hello!" He had a handsome smile. The plaid, collared shirt he was wearing was neatly tucked into a clean pair of khaki pants.

"We're sorry if we frightened you," Barbie apologized.

"Frightened? Me?" The young man laughed. "Not a ghost of a chance! May I help you?"

"We're friends of Mr. Willow's," Barbie explained. "We're going to help out in the garden."

"Well, seeing as I'm the gardener," the man said with a smile, "I guess I should say thank you, then. I'm Kip Mackenzie." He offered his hand to Barbie to shake.

Barbie swallowed hard. *Kip Mackenzie,* she thought. *The man in the museum!*

Chapter 5

- - - - - - - - - - - - - - - - - - -

WHISPERS IN THE WIND

Barbie hid her surprise when the handsome young man said his name. "Nice to meet you, Kip," she said, shaking his hand. "I'm Barbie and this is my friend Becky."

The man shook Becky's hand and smiled. "If there's anything you need, or if you have any questions, just let me know."

"Thanks," Barbie said. As a matter of fact, she did have a question or two. Who was this man called Kip Mackenzie? And why did he want to see the file on Fielding Willow's formulas? She decided to save the questions for another time.

"I have lots to do here," the man continued. "So if you don't mind, I need to get back to work."

"Not at all," Barbie replied. *Was he in a hurry to*

get them out of the shed? Barbie wondered. She and Becky found the tools they needed and took them to the front gardens.

"He seems like a nice guy," Becky remarked. "But did you notice his clothes?"

"Yes, I did," Barbie answered. "He was dressed too neatly for working in the garden."

"Oh, well," said Becky. "At least *we're* dressed for it!"

The two friends worked tirelessly for a few hours. Barbie pulled weeds while Becky pruned the rosebushes. Neither one noticed the heavy black clouds rolling across the sky. Darkness, a loud clap of thunder, and a downpour of rain came without warning.

Mr. Willow threw open the front door and called them inside. He had towels ready for them. "You can dry off in Grandfather's study or any of the guest rooms," he said, pointing to a hallway leading to several rooms. "When you're ready, we'll have a little snack."

Barbie and Becky thanked their host and started down the hallway. As they passed by the study, Barbie stopped. "Oh, Becky, look!" she said. "The wallpaper in this room is beautiful! It's all done in the Fielding rose!"

"Oh, yes!" Becky agreed. "This is the Rose Room. I remember now from one of the exhibits at the museum. Fielding Willow designed this wallpaper just after he created the famous rose."

Barbie stepped inside the room. Everything in the room seemed to be just as Fielding Willow would have left it. On the desk, an old notebook was open and a pair of wire-framed eyeglasses rested on the page. A shelf next to a leather chair was filled with gardening books. Roses covered the walls and ceiling. The room felt warm and cozy. "I can see why Fielding Willow would want to spend so much time here," Barbie commented. "The warm air from the vent feels good after being out in that rain."

"Yes, it does," Becky agreed. "But I'm afraid the vents are ruining the wallpaper. It's peeling so badly. One whole piece is missing."

"Well, we'd better not let our wet clothes drip on any of Fielding Willow's things," said Barbie. "Let's go dry off in the next room."

No sooner had they started down the hallway

again when the lights flickered. Thunder boomed and the sky was lit up with huge bolts of lightning. Becky shrieked and the hallway went completely dark.

"It's all right," Barbie shouted over the noise of the storm. "Don't move, Becky. I'll go back for a flashlight."

"I'm fine," Becky shouted back. "I was just startled by the thunder. I'll stay right here."

Barbie turned and used her hands to feel her way back down the dark hallway. She moved slowly so as not to bump into anything along the way. The wind died down for a few seconds, but Barbie felt a warm breath of air very close to her face. "Who's there?" she said sternly. "Mr. Willow?"

A high-pitched, ghostly voice drifted by her ear. "Fielding," the voice whispered slowly. "F-i-e-l-d-i-n-g! F-i-e-l-d-i-n-g!"

Barbie froze in place. She held her breath and pressed her back to the wall.

Suddenly, a shutter slammed against the house and a strong wind blew in from a window in the nearest room. Another bolt of lightning lit up the room and Barbie saw the curtains blowing at an open window. She rushed to slam it closed, then peered out as a smaller bolt sizzled through the sky. In the flash Barbie caught a glimpse of a mysterious figure running away from the house!

Chapter 6

. . . .

MYSTERIOUS FOOTPRINTS

With one more clap of thunder, the lights in the house came on again. The wind kept blowing and the rain poured down, but the thunder and lightning were moving on. Becky came to the doorway of the room where Barbie stood staring into the darkness. "Are you okay, Barbie?" she asked shakily. "You look as if you've seen a ghost!"

"Maybe I have," Barbie said slowly.

"W-what do you mean?" Becky stammered.

"Barbie? Becky?" Mr. Willow's worried voice called from the living room.

"I'll fill you in later," Barbie whispered to Becky. "I don't want to alarm Mr. Willow just yet. We're coming, Mr. Willow," Barbie called.

The girls didn't see Mr. Willow at first. "Over

here," he said, gasping for breath. He was breathing fast and his fingers gripped the arms of his chair. He looked very frightened. "Someone . . . something . . . I . . . I . . ." he stammered.

"Oh, Mr. Willow," Becky cried. "What happened?"

Mr. Willow took a few deep breaths and again tried to speak. "The lights went out," he said. "I was standing here by the chair. Something brushed against me and forced me backward. Luckily, I fell into the chair."

"Did you see someone?" Barbie asked.

"No one," Mr. Willow replied sadly. "But the force against my shoulder was real, I know it!"

Barbie's eyes went to the old man's shoulder. Part of a dirty handprint marked his shirt. "Mr. Willow," Barbie exclaimed, "someone pushed you!"

"Oh, my gosh!" Becky gasped.

On closer examination, Barbie saw that it wasn't a handprint at all. It was a glove print! The fingers were too wide to be made by a bare hand. But that wasn't the only evidence of dirt. On the floor Barbie saw footprints made by a big shoe.

"Becky," Barbie said more calmly than she felt,

"please wait with Mr. Willow. I'd like to look around if you don't mind, Mr. Willow."

"Of course," Mr. Willow said gratefully. "But please, take a flashlight from the kitchen in case the lights go out again."

While Becky comforted the shaken gentleman, Barbie grabbed a flashlight and examined the prints more closely. The rounded toes and heavy heels told her they were made by boots. The dirt was black, dry, and crumbly. It was more like potting soil than plain dirt. And kneeling down next to them, Barbie noticed the prints had a sweet, musty smell. She traced the footprints backward to the place where the floor met the wall in Fielding Willow's study. The wall was covered with wallpaper, but there was no door. It actually looked as if the footprints had come right through the wall! *Strange*, thought Barbie. *The footprints are definitely from a person, but only a ghost could walk through walls!*

Next, Barbie followed the footprints forward. They led to the bedroom where she had slammed the window shut. Barbie looked out. The rain had stopped and the sky was clearing. Becky and Mr. Willow were busy in the kitchen. Barbie quietly slipped out the front door and walked around to the back of the house. Just as she suspected, there were footprints in the garden under the window. They pointed toward the garden shed. Barbie picked up the garden shovel she'd been using and headed for the shed.

The door was closed tight. Barbie peeked through the windows. She knocked and tried the handle at the same time. No one answered the door, but the knob turned easily in her hand.

"Hello?" Barbie called out as she stepped inside. No answer.

"Anyone home?" she called out again. Her eyes quickly scanned the place. Everything except the boots looked the same as it had earlier! They were no longer by the door. Now they were by the worktable, with a pair of dirty garden gloves next to them. They were covered in fresh, wet mud! At that moment, Barbie thought things did not look good for the gardener. Things only got worse for him when Barbie looked on the worktable and saw a piece of paper with KIP MACKENZIE printed at the top. The words written on the paper looked very familiar to Barbie.

Fielding Formula Part 1

Soil N   Soil Test Potassium, p

Yield N Bray-I 0-40   41-80 81-120 121-160   161+

Nitrogen recommendation = 0.05 YG - STN* + SDA – PCC

(Bray-I) Phosphate recommendation = (0.0225-0.0011 STP)YG

It had been copied from the page in Fielding Willow's notebook! Under the formula writing there was another note:

PICK UP FORMULA FILE FROM VIOLET LANGLEY 4:30 P.M. TELEPHONE: 555-2620, ADDRESS: 25 PINE STREET

"*Violet Langley?*" Barbie said aloud. "She's the woman who took out Fielding Willow's formula file!"

The clock on the wall said 3:25 P.M. Barbie copied down Violet Langley's phone number and address on a scrap of paper. She slipped it into her pocket. As she was about to leave, Barbie saw something she hadn't noticed before. The floorboards next to the muddy boots were loose.

"Aha!" Barbie exclaimed, bending down for a closer look. To her amazement, there was a trap-door in the floor! She pulled up the door in the floor and shone the light on a ladder leading to a dirt floor. "Oh, well," she said, backing down the ladder. "Here goes nothing!"

Chapter 7

· ·

THE SECRET TUNNEL

Barbie's feet touched a hard dirt floor at the bottom of the ladder. The flashlight's beam reached far down a dark hall. "It's a tunnel!" Barbie gasped. She took a deep breath and started down the tunnel. The walls were made of hard, thick dirt. Wooden beams held the roof and sides in place. Barbie wasn't sure what direction she was heading in. The tunnel twisted and turned. Finally, she came to the end. A small wooden door blocked her passage.

Slowly, Barbie pushed the door in. A strong blast of sweet, musty air hit her in the face. It was the same strange odor that drifted through the vents in the house! *Where am I?* Barbie wondered, stepping onto a softer dirt floor.

She shone the flashlight into the dark opening, then realized she didn't need it. Long heat lamps hung from the ceiling over rows of tables holding hundreds of small plants! On the opposite side there were tables of plants growing inside a refrigerated glass case. To Barbie's surprise, the plants were the same in both the heated and the cooled areas! She'd thought that was impossible. Then she noticed something pinned to the wall. It was something Barbie had seen before: part 1 of the Fielding formula!

The dirt floor had freshly dug holes scattered here and there. Footprints close in size to Barbie's feet were everywhere. The prints inside the house were much larger. And one other thing Barbie noticed about these smaller prints — there was a triangle shape on the heel.

Barbie picked up a handful of the dark, dry dirt. It was not ordinary dirt, it was planting soil that had a strong, sweet, musty odor! "Just like the prints on the floor in the house," Barbie whispered to herself.

Suddenly, she remembered the Willow's Way house plan she'd seen at the museum. On it there was a basement area labeled LABORATORY. Barbie was sure she had discovered Fielding Willow's secret laboratory! *But who in the world is using it now?* she wondered.

Barbie searched the big room and found a stone staircase leading up to a dead end. Barbie climbed the stairs. At the top she came to a wooden wall. When she pushed a small button on the wall, it opened to a brighter space covered with rose-patterned wallpaper. She was in Fielding Willow's study!

"Barbie!" Becky and Mr. Willow said together when they saw her. "Where did you come from?"

"I've been down in your basement, Mr. Willow," Barbie exclaimed.

"Basement?" he said. "But there is no basement in this house!"

Mr. Willow wanted to see for himself, but the wall had closed behind Barbie. He and Becky watched in amazement as Barbie placed her hands flat on the wall and moved them across the flowered paper. In seconds, she found what she was looking for. She pressed her fingers against a seam where two panels of wallpaper met. The wall slid open again, and the strong smell from below drifted into the foyer again. "That smell that comes through the vents is from the dirt on the floor of the basement. It appears to be more like potting soil than just ordinary dirt."

"How did you find this secret door in the wall?" Becky asked.

"I think there are a lot of secrets in Willow's Way," Barbie said mysteriously. "Believe it or not, I got into the basement through a tunnel that begins under the garden shed!"

Mr. Willow sat back down in the chair he'd fallen into before. He looked confused. "I'm afraid I don't understand," he said softly. "A tunnel from the garden shed? But why?"

"I think your grandfather was the only one who could have explained that," Barbie said. "There's a laboratory under the house here," she explained.

"Grandfather's laboratory?" Mr. Willow asked in disbelief.

Barbie put her hand on the man's shoulder. "Mr. Willow," she said seriously, "someone is growing plants down there. There are plants under heat lamps and plants in freezing temperatures."

"That's Grandfather's experiment!" Mr. Willow said, turning pale.

"Yes," Barbie agreed. "Someone is trying to finish what your grandfather began. And that person has been coming in and out of your house through the tunnel!"

Barbie closed the secret door in the wall. She moved a chest of drawers in front of it to block the entrance. "Just to be safe," she explained.

"Who would do this?" Becky asked.

"Someone who is interested in gardens and plants," Mr. Willow said.

"And someone who is interested in money," Barbie added. "If your grandfather's secret formula for growing plants in all temperatures was discovered, it could make someone very wealthy."

"You're right, Barbie," Mr. Willow said. "Come to think of it, that new gardener, Kip Mackenzie, has asked a lot of questions about the roses."

Hearing Kip Mackenzie's name reminded Barbie of the scrap of paper in her pocket. She looked at her watch. "Becky," Barbie said excitedly, "it's four o'clock now. Please stay here with Mr. Willow until I get back. I have to leave right away for an appointment in town. I'll explain later."

Becky agreed. She and Mr. Willow watched from the doorway as Barbie drove off to an appointment with someone else who seemed to be interested in Fielding Willow's formulas — Violet Langley.

Chapter 8

• • • • • • • • • • • • • • • • • • • •

VIOLET'S SECRET FORMULA

The roads were slick from the rain, so Barbie drove slowly back to town. Pine Street was in the older section of town. It was where artists had their studios. Each tiny house was painted a different color. Starting on the corner, the houses were blue, orange, green, red, and yellow. The last house was a lovely shade of violet. Barbie read the sign hanging beneath the mailbox: VIOLET'S DESIGN STUDIO, SPECIALIZING IN VINTAGE INTERIOR DESIGN, 25 PINE STREET.

As Barbie pulled up in front of the house, Kip Mackenzie was backing out of the driveway. He sped off toward Main Street and didn't look back.

Barbie thought about following the gardener. She changed her mind when a slender young woman dressed in lavender stepped out onto the porch.

"Hello!" Barbie said, getting out of her car. "I'm Barbie Roberts, a reporter for the *Willow Gazette*," she introduced herself. "You must be Violet Langley."

"Yes, I am," the young woman replied. "You're a reporter? Are you here to see me?"

"I was actually looking for Kip Mackenzie," Barbie said. "I see I just missed him."

"Yes," Violet Langley replied. "You just missed Dr. Mackenzie. He was in quite a hurry to catch up with someone who had just left right before he arrived."

Barbie couldn't hide her surprise. "Did you say Dr. Mackenzie?" she asked. "I didn't know he was a doctor."

"Yes," Violet said, "but he's not the kind of doctor you're thinking of. He explained to me that he holds a doctorate degree in botany, a PhD. So he's Dr. Mackenzie. And you came here to talk to him?" she asked.

"Yes," Barbie replied. "I believe he and I are both

interested in a certain file from the Willow History Museum."

"You and everyone else, it seems," said Violet. "First Mr. Lexa, then Dr. Mackenzie, and now you. But I suppose once you see the file you'll be as disappointed as the other two were."

"Disappointed?" Barbie asked. "What do you mean?"

"The file contains all the color formulas Fielding Willow used in his wallpaper designs. Mr. Lexa seemed very angry when he found that out."

"Color formulas for wallpaper designs!" Barbie exclaimed. "That *is* a surprise!"

"You may as well come inside my studio and see the file, too," Violet said.

Barbie followed Violet Langley inside the house. She was pleasantly surprised by the splashes of color everywhere. Tubes of paints and brushes of all sizes covered one table. Heavy books filled with wallpaper samples were spread out across the desk and shelves. There were also stacks of magazines showing beautifully designed rooms.

"As you can see," Violet explained, "I'm an artist. Mr. Willow hired me to make new paper to patch

42

the spot where this old paper peeled off the wall in the Rose Room." She held up the piece of wallpaper that was missing from the wall in Fielding Willow's study.

"I must have the exact formula for the perfect rose color," Violet continued. "Otherwise, I'll never be able to match it. Thank goodness Fielding Willow saved all of his color formulas. The museum keeps them in the Fielding Willow's formulas file."

"May I see that piece of wallpaper?" Barbie asked, trying not to sound too excited.

"Of course," Violet replied. "But be careful with it. It's very fragile."

Barbie handled the paper gently. The roses were hand painted and the colors were quite unusual. Barbie turned the wallpaper piece over. The color had soaked through, and there was faded writing under the color. Barbie recognized it as Fielding Willow's own handwriting. The words read, *Fielding Formula Part 2.*

"Oh, my gosh!" Barbie exclaimed. "Has anyone else seen this piece of paper?"

"Yes," said Violet. "Mr. Lexa saw it. In fact, he looked at it for quite a long time. I was worried he

43

would tear it. I told him to be careful with it because the warm breeze blowing up from the vent in the Rose Room has made it very brittle."

"Warm breeze blowing in the Rose Room," Barbie repeated slowly. She knew that phrase from somewhere. She took out her notebook and quickly skimmed her notes. At last she found what she was looking for — the line she had copied from Fielding Willow's diary in the glass case at the museum. *Part 2 of my formula shall be safe where roses grow and warm breezes blow.*

Barbie's eyes lit up with excitement. "That's it!" she cried. "I think I know where the formula is!"

"Now that's *really* funny," Violet Langley said. "Mr. Lexa said exactly the same thing!"

"And I'll bet he and Kip Mackenzie are headed for the same place!" Barbie gasped. Immediately, she thought of Becky and Mr. Willow. They might be in *great* danger. "Ms. Langley," she said, "if you don't hear from me in twenty minutes, you must call the police. Send them to Willow's Way. And Ms. Langley," Barbie added urgently, "tell them to hurry!"

Chapter 9

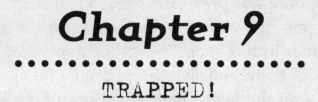

TRAPPED!

Barbie stuck to the speed limit on the drive back to Willow's Way, but her mind was racing. The story for the *Willow Gazette* was supposed to have been a simple piece about the Willow family history. But history had turned to mystery, and Barbie was caught up in it.

Everything looked peaceful when she arrived at Willow's Way. *Maybe I was wrong,* she thought. *Maybe Lexa and Mackenzie weren't coming here at all.*

Then she saw the cars back by the garden shed. A brown car was parked on the side of the shed. Kip Mackenzie's car was in front of the shed, and the passenger door was left wide open.

Barbie's heart pounded. She didn't stop at the house. Instead, she drove halfway to the shed and parked her car. Being careful not to make noise, Barbie dashed the rest of the way to the shed.

The door was open. She peeked in first and saw two sets of wet footprints leading to the open trapdoor in the floor. One set of prints was very large and the smaller set had an odd triangle shape on the heels. Barbie had seen both kinds of footprints before. It surprised her now to see them together. *Are Lexa and Mackenzie working together?* she wondered.

One thing she knew for sure — both men had gone down into the tunnel. She could hear their voices. She had to get to the bottom of this *now*. Taking a deep breath, Barbie stepped down the ladder. Without a flashlight there was nothing to do but feel her way through the tunnel. As she got closer, the voices got louder. They were arguing.

"Get outta my way, Mackenzie!" one man shouted. "That formula is mine! As soon as I have part two, I'll be able to make plenty of planting soil just like the soil we're standing on now."

"So, you've figured out that the secret is in the soil mixture, eh?" Mackenzie said. "You'll never get away with this, Axel."

Axel? Barbie wondered. *Who's Axel?* In her mind, she ran through the list of names in her notebook. *Alfred Willow, Fielding Willow, Carl Axel, Violet Langley, Kip Mackenzie, John Lexa.* "Lexa," she repeated slowly. "Lexa. Lexa spelled backward is Axel! Is John Lexa really this Axel guy? If he is, he must be related to Carl Axel, the assistant that Fielding fired!"

"I've been waiting years to get my hands on the rest of the formula," Axel said angrily. "It's worth millions of dollars, and now that I know where it is, I'm going to take it!"

"Your grandfather was fired by Fielding Willow for doing the same thing you're doing — stealing!" Kip Mackenzie said. "Do you really think the people at my university laboratory would pay you for a formula that isn't even yours? That formula belongs to Alfred Willow now. And the university sent me here to make sure that he gets it."

Now Barbie understood everything. It was Axel who had tried to scare Mr. Willow out of his own house by making him think it was haunted. He must have borrowed Kip's boots and worn them inside Mr. Willow's house. Axel wanted to find part two of Fielding's formula and sell it! This information was enough to put John Axel in jail for years. All Barbie had to do was get out of the tunnel and call the police to finish the job she'd started.

Barbie turned to go back. As she did, a board from the tunnel's ceiling fell. Dirt and cobwebs crumbled down on her face. She screamed, and the two men came running. "It's you!" Axel shouted, pulling Barbie into the laboratory. He laughed in her face. "Barbie Roberts, Reporter! Well, you've got your story now, don't you? But you're not going to have a chance to print it."

"Let go of her, Axel," Kip Mackenzie ordered, pushing the man down onto the floor. Axel picked up a handful of the black dirt and threw it at Kip.

Barbie saw her chance to escape. She couldn't go back through the tunnel. Instead, she ran for the stone steps, shouting, "Becky! Mr. Willow! Open the wall! Open the wall!"

Suddenly, a bright light hit her in the face as the wall opened up. "Barbie!" Becky cried when she saw her friend. "What happened to you?"

To her surprise and great relief, Becky, Mr. Willow, Violet Langley, and two policemen were in

Fielding Willow's study to greet her. "Down there!" Barbie cried, pointing to the basement. Before the police could get to the steps, John Axel came through the door in the wall, with Kip Mackenzie right behind him.

"Arrest that man!" Barbie said, pointing at John Axel. "He's a thief!"

They lost no time in handcuffing the man and taking him away. Amid cheers and congratulations, Barbie thanked Violet Langley for bringing the police. Then, she dug out her notebook and began telling her story, fact by fact, to everyone.

Kip Mackenzie explained what he knew. "I'm from the university," he said. "I work as a botanist, just like Fielding Willow. One day I received a letter from John Axel. He said he was very close to discovering part two of Fielding Willow's secret soil formula. He wanted to sell it to the university for a huge sum of money. The fact is, I had been studying Fielding Willow's work, and I knew the formula was missing."

"And it still *is* missing!" Mr. Willow said.

Barbie smiled. While the others watched, Barbie walked over to the place "where roses grow and warm breezes blow." She stood by the vent and carefully peeled back the already loosened piece of wallpaper. Barbie stepped aside so everyone could see in Fielding Willow's own handwriting,

Fielding Formula Part 2

lb/a	lb/acre-2'	- - - - lb P2O5/acre - - - -				
1000	50	20 15 10 0 0				
1500	75	30 20 15 0 0				
2000	100	40 30 20 10 0				
2500	125	50 35 25 10 0				
Soil N		Soil Test Potassium, ppm				
plus	VL	L M H				
fertilizer						
Yield N	Bray-I 0-40	41-80	81-120	121-160		161+

Kip Mackenzie looked closely at the formula. "Yes!" he exclaimed. "This really *is* the missing part of the formula!"

"And I want you and the university to have the formula and develop it further," Mr. Willow announced. "I shall divide the money earned from the formula between the university and the Willow Museum of History."

"Thank you, Mr. Willow," Kip Mackenzie said sincerely. "The university will be proud to carry on the work of Fielding Willow!"

"My grandfather would be very happy today," Mr. Willow said with tears in his eyes. "He wanted this formula to be shared with the world. Thanks to you, Barbie, his wishes will come true!"

"And thanks to you, Mr. Willow," Becky added, "the museum will be able to keep the history of the whole family alive."

"And thanks to all of you," Barbie said, "I've got a great story for the *Willow Gazette*." She smiled at her friends and they all laughed together.

Barbie's Reporter's Notebook

Can YOU solve *The Haunted Mansion Mystery*? Read the notes in Barbie's Reporter's Notebook. Collect more notes of your own. Then YOU solve it!

Story Assignment: It's the town of Willow's 100th Founder's Day celebration. Write about the history of Willow and its founder, Fielding Willow.

● ● ● ● ● ● ● ● ● ● ● ● ● ● ● ● ● ● ● ●

Background Info

• Fielding Willow, a respected botanist, experimented with plants. He created the Fielding rose. He also designed original wallpaper showing his favorite flowers. The town was named after him 100 years ago.

• Alfred Willow is the grandson of Fielding Willow and lives at the family estate, Willow's Way.

• Carl Axel was Fielding's aide. Fielding fired Carl when he discovered that Carl was selling his formulas to an independent laboratory. Soon after, Fielding became very ill.

• Fielding Willow died just before he finished his last and most important study. The valuable secret project he was working on apparently died with him.

The Mystery

Who: Who is scaring Mr. Alfred Willow?

What: What does the "ghost" want? Alfred Willow reports footsteps, voices, and a strong odor in his grandfather's study.

How: How did the "ghost" get inside the house?

Where: Where is part 2 of Fielding's formula?

Why: Why was the stranger listening to Barbie and Becky at the Willow Café?

Write in the facts and clues you detected in the story. Here are a few to get you started.

- A strange man eavesdropping on Barbie and Becky at the Willow Café rushes out. He leaves a napkin with the address of Willow's Way and the time of Barbie's appointment.
- Willow's Way was designed and built by Fielding Willow in 1870. The floor plan of the house shows many rooms, including a basement area marked LABORATORY.

_____

_____

_____

_____

Jot down the suspects in the case:

Now YOU solve it! Write down the name of the culprit and why you think you have the right person.

_____

_____

_____

_____

_____

_____

_____

_____

_____

_____

_____

_____

_____

_____

_____

_____

_____

_____

_____

_____

CONGRATULATIONS from BARBIE! You are an Official Star Reporter and Mystery Solver! Sharpen your mystery-solving wits and get ready to help Barbie solve her next big case, *The Mystery of the Jeweled Mask*.